Lisa Dillane

Jensen and the Planet

Nightingale Books

NIGHTINGALE PAPERBACK

A CIP catalogue record for this title is
available from the British Library.

ISBN 978-1-83875-938-4

Nightingale Books is an imprint of
Pegasus Elliot MacKenzie Publishers Ltd.
www.pegasuspublishers.com

First Published in 2024

Nightingale Books
Sheraton House Castle Park
Cambridge England

Printed & Bound in Great Britain

Dedication

This book is dedicated to my grandson Jensen, all of the grandchildren that I have yet to meet and my wonderful family.

Jensen looked out of his window
On a warm and sunny
winters day
His heart felt full of total joy
To go outside and play

The winter leaves were falling
Brown and orange to the ground
He would entwine and
blend together
To make a Jensen crown

He was excited too for Christmas
That was not so far away
With its joy and songs and love
and hope
A most special King of days

For now though it was playtime
And he dressed to go outside
He would run and jump and twirl
and dance
And sometimes he would hide

Jensen called out to his mummy
Oh, I know what we should do
We should call and ask if Tommy
Would like to come and play here too

Tommy was his best friend
They had known each other long
From the nursery to the playground
They had sung the friendship song

Mummy laughed and said
oh Jensen
You are super mates it's clear
But as mummy turned to make
the call
Jensen thought he saw a tear

Tommy came at once
for playtime
Like a greyhound out the traps
They had sandwiches
at lunch time
And for dinner black bean wraps

In winter sun sets early
So, the days are rather short
Twilight loomed spectacular
As daylight drew to halt

Oh my what fun we have
had today
Said Jensen to his mate
We've laughed and run
and painted stones
And swung upon the gate

The sun had shone so boldly
So, their paintings were quite dry
Jensen said let's show my mum
our stones
But Tommy was so shy

Jensen bolstered Tommy's
heart up
Said his works no less than great
Mummy smiled and so agreed
But then she said, it's getting late

As Tommy said his long goodbyes
His daddy waiting by the door
Jensen shouted goodbye friend
The best day that's for sure

So, after play and supper
Jensen snuggled cosy down
He turned his head to mummy
And just caught the smallest frown

Okay, said Jensen quite bravely
As his daddy came to sit
I know that somethings not
quite right
So, mummy, what is it?

His parents looked at Jensen
And as unity they sighed
Mummy said, I'm sorry Jensen
You were not meant to see me cry

My thoughts today were on
the planet
And how everything's in change
A warm and sunny winter's day
Is nothing if not strange

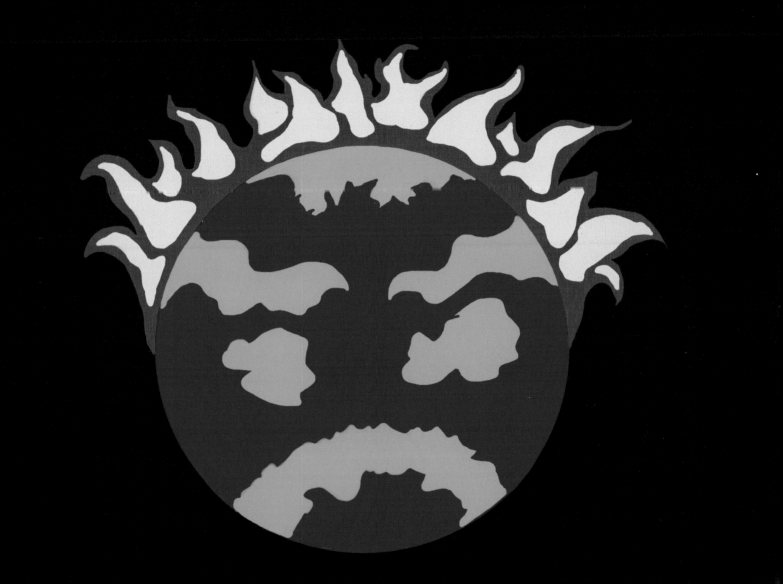

You will learn at school about this
How humanity's to blame
Why the actions that we are taking
Means that nothing stays the same

Winter should be cold and snowy
The leaves fallen and long gone
When the sun has got his hat on
Then somethings really wrong

It's not for you to worry
But it's something you should hear
Now it's time to save our planet
And we can without a fear

So all the little children
Can help in very many ways
We can love and nourish
our planet
Each and every single day

You can get to know our
mother earth
By spending time outdoors
By relishing in nature
And wondering at our shores

You can shower in 5 minutes
And turn your lights from high to low
You can recycle clothes and
books and toys
There are so many ways to go

By using lower energy
Our carbon footprint will be less
And that in time delivers
Reduced planet harm and stress

Then maybe winters will
be winters
And our summers warm
and bright
We will have spring and autumn
once again
And unpolluted nights

I like the thought of this
said Jensen
Reusing things each day
I can tell my friends to join
our club
Will teacher have a say?

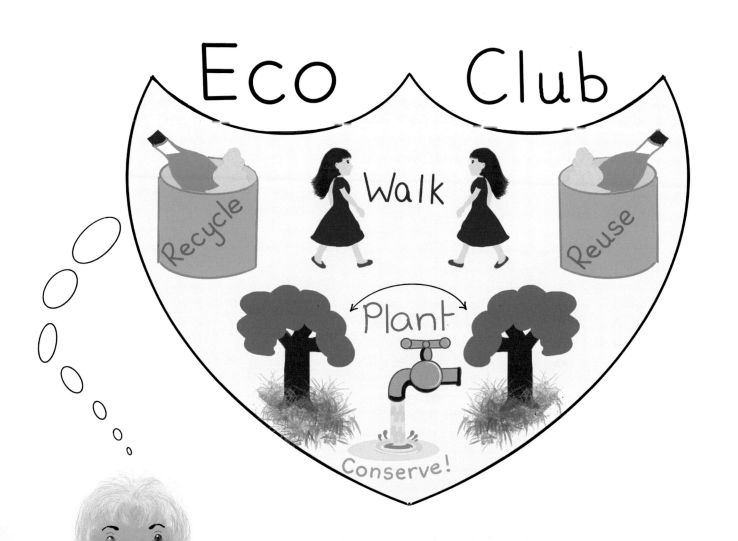

Oh yes said mummy gladly
There will be lots to learn
from school
But now you know the basics
You might understand it all

arbon
ioxide
missions
ssil
uels
ea
evel
OP 26
arth
top
Environment!
Save
Our
World ☺
Plastic
Recycle
I want to help save our World.
Jensen

Right said Jensen wisely
From now on I shall be
An eco-friendly warrior
Tommy too, just wait and see

That's perfect said his daddy
One small step at a time
From little acorns oak
trees grow
Said Jensen quite sublime

So, there we have it children
We all have much to do
But if we all follow Jensen
We can make our dreams
come true!

About the Author

After many years working in a corporate environment, the birth of my first grandchild filled me with wonder and inspired me to do something very different. I hope that, in a small way, this book will inspire him and hopefully many other children, to look for small ways that they can help our planet. The book is designed to discuss a serious subject without fear and through the fun of poetry.

Acknowledgements

To Glen from Apple who supported me to explore a drawing tablet for the illustrations and to my husband William who encourages me always.